A Random House book
Published by Random House Australia Pty Ltd
Level 3, 100 Pacific Highway, North Sydney NSW 2060
www.randomhouse.com.au

First published by Random House Australia in 2015

Random House Books is part of the Penguin Random House group of
companies whose addresses can be found at global.penguinrandomhouse.com

National Library of Australia
Cataloguing-in-Publication Entry

Creator: Darlison, Aleesah, author
Title: Awesome animal stories for kids / Aleesah Darlison; illustrator James Hart
ISBN: 9780857989680 (pbk)
Target audience: For children
Subjects: Animals – Juvenile fiction
         Children's stories
Other Creators/Contributors: Hart, James, illustrator
Dewey Number: A823.4

Cover illustration and design by James Hart
Cover design by Leanne Beattie
Typeset in 14.5/24pt New Baskerville by Midland Typesetters, Australia
Printed in Australia by Griffin Press, an accredited ISO AS/NZS 14001:2004
Environmental Management System printer

Random House Australia uses papers that are natural, renewable and recyclable
products and made from wood grown in sustainable forests. The logging
and manufacturing processes are expected to conform to the environmental
regulations of the country of origin.

Written by

ALEESAH DARLISON

Illustrated by

JAMES HART

RANDOM HOUSE AUSTRALIA

FOREWORD

I love animals. Big ones. Little ones. Fantasy ones.
Furry ones. Feathered ones. Scaly ones.

Animals are awesome.

I suppose it all goes back to my childhood
growing up in the country. I always had animals
around me. And I don't mean my brother and sisters,
although they did get rather wild at times. I mean the
ones we had on our farm – horses, cows, dogs, cats,
ducks, rabbits, chickens, guineafowl, you name it.

And then, of course, there were the native animals
in the bush – kangaroos, wallabies, koalas, possums,
snakes, echidnas, goannas . . . Did I mention snakes?
There were lots of those!

I learned a lot about animals as a kid. I learned
how to care for them, how to appreciate their special

and unique qualities and how we should protect them and their native habitats.

Now that I'm grown-up, I get to write stories about those animals that I love so much. Combining my passion for writing and my love of animals really is the best job in the world!

Being able to write this collection of animal stories was a dream come true. I got to draw on some of my experiences from my childhood. I got to give my imagination a workout, creating stories about unusual and out-of-this-world fantasy animals. I got to write important stories about caring for baby animals. Best of all, I got to write some outrageously funny stories about animals, too. Those were probably my favourite stories to write.

Like creating the perfect pizza with all the best toppings, I've tried to create the perfect mix of awesome animal stories for kids to read. There's a combination of funny and serious, clever and silly, realistic and fantastic stories in this book so young readers can experience a wide range of themes, ideas, settings, plots, twists and, of course, animals. My aim was to entertain, enlighten, challenge and delight readers as they savoured these amazing animal stories.

Having James Hart's illustrations sprinkled throughout the book helps bring my stories to life and adds an extra layer of storytelling. I hope you have as much fun reading these awesome animal stories as I did writing them.

Happy reading!
Aleesah Darlison

CONTENTS

PIG-NAPPED!

King Pig was the wise and kind ruler of a rich pigdom called Pigdonia. He lived in Pigdonia with his wife, Queen Pig, and their daughter, Princess Pigletta. The royal family was loved and respected by all their loyal subjects.

King Pug was the vain and silly ruler of the pugdom called Pugenborg, which was right next door to Pigdonia. Because he was vain and silly, King Pug spent all his time eating cupcakes and playing dress-ups. His favourite costume was a unicorn. He would tape an ice-cream cone to his forehead, tie tassels to his paws and tail and roll in pink glitter before prancing around the castle, snorting and neighing.

King Pug really didn't think about anyone or anything but himself – except when it came to riches.

While tourists flocked to Pigdonia to admire its stunning natural wonders, no one visited Pugenborg with its hot deserts, rocky coastlines and rundown towns. Pigdonia grew richer. The pigdom flourished. But on the other side of the border, Pugenborg grew poorer.

King Pug was extremely jealous of King Pig. He was also lonely and bored and, unlike King Pig, had no family to love him or temper his silliness.

'I need a plan to bring that pompous King Pig down,' King Pug decided. 'What will hurt him the most?' He gazed out his window, over the wall into Pigdonia and spotted Princess Pigletta playing in the rose garden. 'Aha!' he cried. He knew what he would do.

That night, when all was still, King Pug dressed for his mission. He squeezed into his new black tracksuit and zipped it up. He pulled on his black socks and matching black running shoes. He picked up his black beanie, cut a hole in it so that he could see out, then tugged it down over his head to hide his face.

He was about to leave when he spotted his pot of glitter on the dressing table.

'A little glitter can't hurt,' King Pug murmured as he sprinkled several pawfuls of purple and gold sparkles over himself. He glanced in the mirror and liked what he saw. 'Very regal, your majesty,' he told his reflection.

King Pug snuck out of his castle. He took a ladder from the royal garden shed and propped it up against the wall that separated Pigdonia from Pugenborg. He clambered up the ladder, sat on the brick wall, swung the ladder over to the other side, and climbed down into King Pig's garden.

King Pug crept through the garden to the castle. He passed a sleeping guard at the castle door and padded along the hallway to Princess Pigletta's bedroom.

The princess was fast asleep. King Pug placed a ransom note on her bedside table, wrapped Princess Pigletta in her bedspread and lifted her gently off the bed.

'Rather . . . heavy . . .' he gasped, teetering and tottering under the princess's weight before he steadied his little pug legs.

He carried Princess Pigletta out of the palace, up the ladder, over the brick wall, down the ladder on the other side and towards his castle, panting and puffing all the way.

————

When Princess Pigletta woke in the morning, she found herself in King Pug's dungeon, deep beneath his castle. She had no idea where she was. When she squealed for help, no one heard her.

Poor Princess Pigletta was afraid.

Meanwhile, her father and mother next door in Pigdonia were reading the ransom note.

'Your pigdom for a pig!' the note said. 'Pack up and leave your palace by noon tomorrow and I will release Pigletta. Ignore my demands and you will never see your daughter again. You have been paw-warned.'

'I don't understand who could do such a thing,' said Queen Pig, sobbing into her handkerchief.

'Nor do I,' said King Pig, 'but I *do* know that I won't be giving up my darling Pigletta *or* my wonderful pigdom. Search the palace!' he commanded his guards. 'Search the grounds! You must find Pigletta!'

But even though the guards searched everywhere in Pigdonia, they could not find the princess.

'What are we to do?' King Pig gasped, collapsing onto his throne.

'Wait a minute. I know someone who can help.' Queen Pig stopped sobbing. She rummaged through her desk and handed her husband a card. 'I've heard this human does great work.'

**Got a crime to solve
or a mystery to unravel?**

Call Liberty Rose, Private Eye

Phone: 1800 DETECT

'Bring this private eye to me right away,' King Pig told his butler.

'Well,' said Liberty Rose, 'I must begin my investigation somewhere. I will start in Princess Pigletta's bedroom.'

The private eye ran her finger along Princess Pigletta's pillow, the bedside table and the door handle.

'Interesting . . .' she murmured. She held her finger up to study what had stuck to it. A single speck of purple glitter flashed in the sunlight that was shining in through the window.

Liberty Rose strode down the hallway and out the door. King Pig and Queen Pig followed closely behind.

The private eye bent down to study the flagstones that surrounded the palace. She ran her finger over those, too. A tiny fleck of gold caught the light.

'Was Princess Pigletta in the habit of wearing glitter?' she asked.

'No,' King Pig said. 'She hated the stuff. She has a very sensitive nose, you see. Glitter makes her sneeze. We banned it from the palace.'

'Then I would suggest that our pig-napper was wearing glitter when he or she took your daughter,' Liberty Rose said. 'Gold and purple glitter, to be precise.'

Liberty Rose followed the trail of glitter leading to the wall. 'I'll need a ladder,' she told King Pig's butler, who scurried off to get one.

When the butler returned, Liberty Rose, King Pig and Queen Pig climbed over the wall and into King Pug's garden.

'Ahem!' Liberty Rose coughed.

King Pug was dozing on his deckchair, sunbaking beside his pool. Specks of glitter in his fur sparkled in the sunlight.

'Excuse me, your majesty,' Liberty Rose said.

King Pug sat bolt upright. 'Who are you? What are you all doing in my garden?'

'I'm Liberty Rose, Private Eye, and these are your royal neighbours, King Pug and Queen Pug. We're here to investigate the pig-napping of Princess Pigletta from Pigdonia, the pigdom next door.'

'I don't know anything about that,' King Pug said, coolly sipping his pineapple juice.

'Oh, but I think you do.' Liberty Rose handed the smug pug a piece of paper. 'And I have a warrant here issued by the High Court that says I can search through any and all castles in the region to look for Princess Pigletta.'

King Pug looked uncomfortable. 'The High Court?' he said, gulping.

'Yes.' Liberty Rose nodded.

'All right, then,' King Pug said, his eyes shifting from left to right. He really wanted to run away but he thought that might be unbecoming for a king.

Liberty Rose, King Pig and Queen Pig followed the trail of glitter into King Pug's castle and down to the dungeons. As they neared the room where Princess Pigletta was being held captive, they heard squealing.

'Princess Pigletta!' King Pig cried. He rushed forward, breaking open the lock with his strong trotters and opening the door. Little Princess Pigletta was so happy to see her parents that she ran straight into their open arms. Tears spilled down the cheeks of the happy family as they were reunited.

———

The High Court decreed that King Pug was to pay for his naughtiness by going to work as the court jester for King Pig. At first, King Pug was furious with the ruling but once he'd performed several gigs at King Pig's court, he couldn't help but enjoy himself.

He *loved* being the court jester. After all, he got to dress up in glorious outfits and he was always the centre of attention.

As for King Pig and his family, they too were thrilled with the arrangement because they got to know their neighbour better and they had free entertainment every day. They also knew that from now on their darling Princess Pigletta would be safe. Now they really could live happily ever after.

NIGEL'S GREAT ESCAPE

'Oh no!' I heard a cry from downstairs.
'Nigel's missing!'

Those words were the ones we all
feared. Another Nigel escape was the last
thing we needed. Sure enough . . .

'Action stations, everyone.' Mum was
gearing up for a major search, hauling
on her gumboots and gloves to go with
her khaki uniform.

'Alice, get a broom,' Mum told my sister. 'George, fetch a net.'

I ran into the laundry and grabbed the biggest fishing net I could find while Alice ran to the garage to fetch a broom. Even though it was a big net, to me it looked small and flimsy. Nigel would never fit inside.

'Boots on, kids,' Mum said. 'I'd like to avoid a trip to the hospital if possible.' She collected her stick with the loop of rope on the end of it. 'Got everything? Okay, let's go!'

We stood cautiously at the back door, our eyes scanning left and right. Nigel was a fairly relaxed reptile.

As long as he had food.

'When was the last time you fed him, Mum?' I asked.

'Yesterday.' Mum grimaced. 'I think.'

'Great,' I said, sighing. So maybe Nigel wouldn't be so relaxed after all.

Stepping into our backyard was like stepping into a jungle. Mum owned a petting zoo so we had loads of animals. Mum wasn't big on mowing the lawn, either, so the grass was pretty long. Pretty perfect for hiding runaways, too.

'Look!' I pointed to a patch of dirt under the mulberry tree, where the grass never grew. Four slender footprints and the imprint of a tail swish showed. 'Nigel's tracks.'

We followed the tracks towards the fence. Several palings were broken at the bottom.

'I've been meaning to fix that,' Mum said.

Alice groaned. 'That's what you always say.'

I peered over the fence. Usually Mrs Tremble's garden was neat and tidy, with colourful flowerbeds and shipshape vegetable patches.

Not today.

'Uh, guys,' I said. 'Have a look.'

Mum and Alice peered over the fence with me.

'Oh dear,' Mum said.

Through the middle of Mrs Tremble's vegie patch was a messy, winding, Nigel-sized path where dirt and plants had been uprooted.

We tore our eyes away from the mess when we heard the sound of breaking glass inside Mrs Tremble's house, followed by a scream.

Mum and I looked at each other. 'Nigel!'

We leaped over the fence, Alice close on our heels, and raced in through the back door, broom and stick and net flying.

Mrs Tremble was lying on her living-room floor, unconscious.

'She must have fainted,' Alice said.

'Are you sure? Any bite marks?' Mum asked.

Alice checked Mrs Tremble all over. 'Nope.'

'Thank goodness,' Mum said. 'Now, where's Nigel?'

I looked at the front screen door. It had an enormous hole torn through it.

'Um, I think he went that way,' I said, pointing out the door. My hand was shaking. This was not good.

'Alice, you stay here with Mrs Tremble,' Mum said. 'George and I will go after Nigel.'

We left Alice kneeling beside Mrs Tremble and bolted out the door.

'Oh no,' Mum said. 'The front gate is open.'

In the distance we heard screeching tyres and car horns.

'Down there!' Mum cried.

We sprinted along the street and around the corner. At the next intersection cars, trucks and buses were parked at various angles, their motors still running. It looked like there had nearly been an accident.

This was worse than Nigel's last escape. Much worse.

'I'll sort this mess out,' Mum said. She handed me the stick with the rope loop.

'It's up to you now, George. Find Nigel before he causes any more trouble.'

I took off down the street. Past the shopping mall. Past the service station. Past the retirement village where a bunch of elderly people on electric scooters whizzed away.

I saw the flick of a tail.

'Nigel!' I cried. 'Come back!'

Nigel didn't stop and it didn't take me long to realise that he was heading towards the ocean. I could see the beach ahead. He must have been able to smell the salt water.

'Nigel, wait!' I called.

Nigel glanced back at me, then turned a sharp left.

What? He wasn't heading for the water?

I chased him along the sand, towards the stormwater drain that emptied into the sea. It poked out of the sandstone cliffs at the north end of the beach. Its opening was huge, rusty and mossy.

Nigel scrambled inside.

Argh! This was all Mum's fault! If only she'd made sure the cage was shut and that Nigel was fed properly! Then he wouldn't have escaped and I wouldn't have to go crawling into a scary drain after a crocodile.

An image of Mum's face appeared before me. I sighed. Mum worked so hard with her petting zoo. She didn't mean for Nigel to escape. She didn't mean for any of this to happen . . . I had to help Mum. I had to get Nigel back.

I took a deep breath and stepped into the drain. I could hear water dripping down the walls and my boots crunching over the sand and gravel. My heart pounded in my chest.

Finally, my eyes adjusted to the darkness. I saw something moving. No, make that lots of somethings moving. Lots of little somethings with flicking tails and rows of tiny teeth. I tried counting all the heads and tails but there were too many and they wouldn't stay still. I got to twenty and gave up.

More than twenty baby crocodiles.

Curled around them was a much bigger crocodile. A mummy crocodile called Nigel.

Well, I thought, she couldn't be 'Nigel' anymore. She had to be 'Nigella'.

That's why Nigel – I mean, Nigella – was racing down here! She must have come here last time she escaped, to lay her eggs! And now they had hatched, she wanted to be with her babies.

I spotted something else in the darkness. My breath caught in my throat. Behind Nigella was another much, *much* bigger crocodile.

'The daddy crocodile,' I whispered.

Without taking my eyes off him, I slunk backwards out of the drain. I had just reached daylight again when I heard scratching and scraping. Nigella, the daddy crocodile and their babies appeared.

Nigella scuttled over to me. It took all of my courage to stand still. I didn't want to make any sudden movements in case she thought her babies were in danger.

She nudged my sneaker with her snout and looked up at me.

'It's ok-k-kay,' I stuttered. 'Mum will understand. You're making the great escape. You have your little ones to think of.' I smiled. The city would be a dangerous place for her babies.

I still can't believe it, but I swear that Nigella winked at me, as if to tell me she understood and was saying goodbye.

Then she opened her mouth wide. The baby crocodiles scurried towards her and jumped inside. It was kind of weird to see, but I knew that this was how crocodiles carried their young.

With a final tap of her tail, Nigella headed towards the ocean, ignoring the sunbathers who screamed and sprinted away, sending sand flying everywhere. The daddy crocodile followed.

Happily, I watched as the crocodiles dived into the surf, their tails swishing from side to side as they swam away in search of a new home.

I swiped away the tear forming in the corner of my eye. Nigel – I mean, Nigella – had been a good pet. She'd always been kind and patient with the children at parties. I knew she was going to be a great mum, too.

Something on the ground caught my eye. I glanced down. One small, white egg rested in the sand.

'Hey, you forgot . . .' I start to shout.

It was too late. Nigella was gone.

As I picked the egg
up, the shell cracked.
A tiny snout appeared.
The baby crocodile
squeaked and wriggled
in my hands.

I smiled. 'Here we
go again . . .'

ORPHAN FOAL

We knew straightaway there was a
problem with the mare and her new
buckskin foal. He was the cutest foal I'd
ever seen and I loved him at first sight.

But his mother didn't want him.
For some reason, she wouldn't let him
near her.

'Why does she keep doing that,
Dad?' I asked, as we watched the foal

repeatedly sidle up to his mum, and his mum repeatedly kick him away.

'Sometimes it happens, Ella,' Dad said. 'But you watch – the foal will keep trying. He needs to nurse from her. He needs colostrum.'

'What's that?'

'The first milk. Babies need it to protect them from disease. If the foal doesn't get any, he might die.'

In the end, Dad had to milk the mare by hand. Then we squeezed some colostrum down the hungry foal's throat. It was messy and awkward but the foal got some of the precious yellow fluid in the end.

'We'll have to do that every few hours

until he's had enough,' Dad said. 'He needs over a litre if he's going to survive.'

'What about after that?'

'We could rent a nurse mare for the foal, but they're too expensive. We can't afford it.' He looked worried. 'We could hand nurse him, but we're already so busy. I'm not sure we could manage.'

'I'll do it,' I said straightaway.

Mum squeezed my shoulder. 'Being a mum is a big task. He'll need to feed every two hours for the first few weeks, just like a human baby. Are you sure you want that responsibility?'

Tears stung my eyes. 'I'll feed him and take care of him. I'll do anything to save him.'

'Okay,' Dad said. 'Let's give it a go.'

Yes! I hugged Mum and Dad. 'Thank you! Thank you! What will we call him?' I asked as the foal nuzzled my hand.

Mum watched the foal with sad eyes. 'There's no point naming him if he's not going to live. Let's just wait awhile.'

Later, after we'd fed the foal more colostrum, we settled him into the stable. Then we checked Dad's horse books for information about rearing orphan foals.

'It says here that bottle feeding foals can be difficult.' I pointed to the page while Dad leaned over my shoulder.

'Maybe we can teach him to drink from a bowl instead,' Dad suggested, 'like we do with the poddy calves.'

'It's worth a try,' Mum agreed.

'What will he drink?' I asked.

'Formula is good,' said Dad, skimming the page.

Later that morning, Dad bought some formula from the produce store. We mixed the powder with boiling water and once it had cooled, we carried it up to the foal.

Dad poured the milk into a shallow bowl.

'I'll feed him,' I said.

Dad handed me the bowl. 'Good luck, little mother.'

Looping my arm around the foal's neck, I pushed his muzzle into the bowl, sliding my fingers into his mouth to get him sucking. The foal pulled back and skipped away.

'Come on, little one. You must be hungry.' I pushed his head into the bowl again.

This time the foal bunted me. The bowl slipped out of my hand and went flying. The milk dribbled away in the straw, lost.

'Maybe I should try,' Dad said.

'No. I'll do it.'

I poured more milk into the bowl. This time, I braced the foal between my legs.

'Come on.' I pushed the foal's nose into the bowl for the third time. I slipped my fingers into his mouth and wiggled them. He started sucking. *Hard.* I heard him gulp down the milk and felt him swallow.

'He's drinking!' I cried.

The foal quickly got the hang of it. By the afternoon, I didn't even have to use my fingers. Whenever the foal saw the bowl, he would whinny and trot straight to me.

The next day was Monday and I tried getting out of school. 'Can't I stay home until he's older? He needs looking after.'

Mum laughed. 'You'll miss too many lessons. I'll look after your precious baby. Don't worry.'

The day dragged by. When the school bus finally stopped at our gate, I jumped out and bolted home.

'Is he all right?' I asked, bursting through the door.

'He's fine.' Mum smiled and handed me a bowl of warm milk. 'A little hungry, though.'

That first week, whenever I wasn't at school, I was feeding the foal. Every two hours. Even during the night.

At ten days old, I started stretching the foal's feed to every six hours. He was going well, but we still hadn't named him. When I spoke to Dad about it he said, 'Let's wait and see.'

When I came home from school two afternoons later, Mum told me she'd tried to feed him some hay but he'd refused it.

'Maybe he'll take it from me,' I said. I offered the foal a handful of fresh, green hay. He sniffed at it, eyeing it uncertainly.

'Come on, eat up. It's good for you.'

The foal curled his tiny tongue around several strands of hay and pulled them into his mouth. As he nibbled

the strands, his eyes
lit up with delight.
He leaned forward
to take more.
I knew then
that he liked it.

'Good boy.' I rubbed his neck while
he munched away.

The foal started to eat more solid
food and drink less milk.

When he was two weeks old, Dad
surprised me by asking if I'd thought
of a name yet.

I shook my head. Even though I'd
thought about it a lot, I hadn't come
up with a name I liked. 'I can't decide,'
I said.

'Sleep on it tonight and we'll see what the morning brings. It looks like this little guy might make it after all.'

But the next morning, when I went to feed the foal, he didn't trot over to me like usual. Instead he lay slumped in the corner with sunken eyes and wobbly legs. I raced down to the house to tell Dad.

'He's got scours,' Dad said, examining the foal.

'What's that?'

'It's like a stomach virus,' Dad explained. 'The lining of his bowel is damaged and he's losing fluids. We have to be careful he doesn't dehydrate.'

'How did it happen?'

'Maybe he ate something he shouldn't have or drank some contaminated milk. Have you been cleaning his bucket properly?'

I shot Dad a guilty look. 'I think so.' I couldn't remember clearly what I'd done last night. I'd been too exhausted. I felt terrible. What if I'd done something to harm the foal? 'Will he be okay?'

'Let's hope so.'

Luckily it was Sunday so I didn't have to go to school. I changed the bedding in the stall and made sure the foal drank plenty of milk. I also fed him a special drink Dad bought to rehydrate him.

All through the night I sat with the foal. Mum and Dad didn't try to talk me out of it. They knew I wouldn't leave him.

In the morning, the cackling laughter of kookaburras woke me. Picking the hay from my hair, I sat up. Hot, horsey breath tickled my neck. I turned to see the foal standing beside me. He nickered cheekily.

Laughing, I jumped up and hugged him, then raced down to the house for his milk.

'He's okay!' I shouted as I hurtled into the kitchen. Mum and Dad, fresh out of bed, stared at me like I was crazy. I didn't care. All that mattered was that my foal was well again.

Soon he was back to his energetic self and was eating and drinking properly. After that, we all got more sleep.

'Well,' said Dad a few days later, as we gathered around the foal's stall, 'what are you going to call him?'

'Sunny,' I said, 'because of his golden colour and also because raising him has been like having a son.' I giggled. 'Well, kind of.' I clicked my fingers and called, 'Here, Sunny!'

Sunny looked up and skipped over to me for a pat, as if he knew his name already.

'You're mine forever,' I whispered into his ear as I held him tight. 'My little Sunny.'

GO AWAY, YOU CRAZY DOG!

Digby lived in the country. He'd never seen the ocean until one summer when his parents took him on a holiday to the beach.

Digby was so excited! He couldn't believe how clear and blue the water looked, or how warm it felt on his toes.

On the first day of their holiday, while Mum was buying fish and chips for lunch, Digby saw a bright yellow poster taped to a pole.

**Hey kids! Want to win a brand-new bike?
Here's your chance!
Enter the Great Sand Sculpture
Competition.**

Where: Sandy Beach

When: 10 am, Saturday 12 January

Entry fee: $5

Saturday! That was tomorrow!

Digby thought about his clunky old hand-me-down bike back home. The chain was rusty and the handlebars were loose. The seat was torn and the tyres were bald. More than anything, Digby wanted a new bike.

'Dad, look at this. Can I enter?' he asked.

Dad peered at the poster. 'Sure. It looks like fun.'

Mum came back and they all found an empty picnic table where they could sit for lunch. Mum tore open the packet of fish and chips. The smell of hot oil, salt and vinegar wafted on the breeze.

A huge golden labrador trotted towards the table, sniffing the air. He stopped and sat on the grass beside Digby, sticking out his tongue, eyeing the food and wagging his tail.

'Go away.' Mum waved at the dog.

The labrador jumped up. He ran around the picnic table, barking madly and sending seagulls scattering. After his fifth loop of the table, the dog screeched to a halt. He threw himself on the ground and looked up at Digby with pleading eyes.

'Go away, you crazy dog!' Dad shouted.

The dog yapped and wagged his tail.

'Silly dog,' Dad groaned.

Digby felt sorry for the dog. It reminded him of his blue heeler, Lady, back at home. She was such a friendly dog. This dog looked friendly, too. And hungry.

When Mum and Dad weren't looking, Digby tossed the dog a chip. He caught it in his mouth, gulped it down and whined for more.

Digby kept sneaking chips to the dog until all of his were gone.

———

That night, Digby tossed and turned as he dreamed about the brand-new bike. He wanted it so badly!

In his dreams he did backflips, bar spins and barhops. He did pogos, tail whips and elephant glides. He'd never done any of these things before, but anything seemed possible on his new bike.

There was just one problem.

Digby didn't know anything about sand sculptures. He was never going to win the prize.

———

The next morning, as soon as his parents were dressed, Digby hurried them down to the beach where they joined the queue of kids registering for the competition. He was nervous and kept

chewing his fingernails. He still worried
that he wouldn't win the competition,
but he had to try.

'Any idea what you're going to make?'
asked Dad.

Digby squirmed. He had no idea, but
he couldn't tell Dad. 'It's top secret,' he
said finally.

'Oh.' Dad tapped his nose. 'You've got
a plan to blitz them all. That's my boy.'

The line inched forward. When they
reached the check-in table, Dad paid
the entry fee. Digby was given a sticker
to wear. It had '97' printed on it in big
black numbers. He waved goodbye to his
parents and set off for the area marked
as his.

The judge read out the rules over a loudspeaker, then shouted, 'You have one hour starting . . . *now*!'

A bell rang. The competition was on!

All the other kids set to work.

Digby sat on his plot, sifting sand through his hands, trying to think of what to build while avoiding looking at everyone else as they dug and tunnelled, packed and carved.

One boy was building a castle
surrounded by a moat. A girl nearby
was making a mermaid complete with
a seaweed necklace. Another kid was
sculpting a dolphin. All the sculptures
looked good, but Digby wanted to make
something better. Something different.
If only he could think what it was!

'What's he doing?' Mum whispered.

'He'll be fine,' Dad whispered back.
'He's got a plan.'

Digby didn't have a plan. And time
was slipping away.

'Forty-five minutes to go!' came a
voice through the loudspeaker.

Digby felt something furry brush
against his leg. He looked down and

saw the labrador he'd shared his lunch with the day before.

The dog looked up at him, pink tongue lolling. He barked, then started digging on Digby's plot.

'Go away, you crazy dog!' Dad shouted, waving his arms wildly at the dog.

But the labrador stayed put. He dug so quickly that sand piled up into huge mounds. Digby had never seen a dog dig so fast. Then, to Digby's disbelief, the dog sat up on his hind legs and used his front paws to shape the piles of sand.

'Of course!' Digby cried, suddenly struck by an idea. 'Thanks, crazy dog!'

Digby couldn't believe his luck! He

got to work digging and sculpting, right alongside the crazy dog. It was hot in the sun. Sweat poured down his face, but he didn't stop for a single moment.

People standing nearby started to laugh and point at Digby and the dog as they sculpted their sand piles.

One grumpy parent grumbled, 'Are dogs allowed to enter the competition?'

'The judge didn't say they couldn't,' someone else said, remembering the rules that were read out before the competition began.

Digby glanced at the clock.

'Two minutes to go,' he told the dog.

'Woof!' The dog understood. He raced around the plot, carving the sand into all sorts of shapes. Digby was having trouble keeping up.

When there were only ten seconds to go, the whole crowd started counting down. 'Ten, nine, eight . . .'

There was still one more sculpture to build! Digby ran over . . .

'. . . Three, two, one!'

'Tools down!' the judge cried as the buzzer sounded.

'Oh, no,' Digby moaned. He hadn't finished. There was a big hole in the middle of his sculpture. There was no way he could win.

'Never mind,' Mum said. 'You were great. Look, here comes the judge.'

Just then, the labrador lolloped over.

He was soaking wet, as if he'd been swimming in the ocean.

'What's that crazy dog doing now?' Dad said.

The dog rolled in the sand until he was covered, then he ran into the middle of Digby's plot and sat down. Right where the hole was.

The judge strode over to Digby's plot. 'Wow, you've done a lot of work,' he said. 'Not exactly a beach theme, but I like it. I'm always looking for original sculptures.'

Digby smiled and nodded. He pretended not to know that there was a dog sitting right in the middle of his sand sculpture.

The judge tapped his chin with his
pen. 'I must say, that dog looks very real!'

Digby looked puzzled. Couldn't he
tell that the dog *was* real?

The judge waved his clipboard at the
crowd and called for quiet. 'The winner
of the Great Sand Sculpture Competition
– and a new bike – is . . . Digby West, with
his farmyard-themed sculpture, complete
with sheep, cattle, horses and a very
realistic-looking sand dog. Well done,
Digby!'

Everyone clapped politely. Dad and Mum cheered.

Digby turned to look at the dog. He wanted to give him a pat for helping him win the bike, but the shaggy golden labrador was no longer there.

In his place was a dog made of golden sand.

PUFF RETURNS

Deep within a seaside cave, hidden from
prying eyes, a dragon lay slumbering
until one day the sound of laughter
made him stir . . .

'Jack! Don't go in there,' Mum said. 'It could be dangerous.'

'It's fine,' Jack called over his shoulder. 'I'll be out in a minute.'

It really wasn't a day for the beach.

Icy.

Wet.

Windy.

Still, Jack thought it was fun being out of the city, exploring his new home. He laughed as he skipped over the black pebbles littering the entrance to the cave. Jack suddenly stopped. An enormous, dark figure lay huddled on the cave floor.

'Hello!' Jack called cheerily.

The figure remained still and silent.

'Hell*oooooo*!' Jack shouted.

Slowly, reluctantly, the creature opened one large emerald eye to stare at Jack. 'Who are you?' it mumbled, grumpily.

'I'm Jack.'

'Jack? My Jackie?' The creature lifted its head for a closer look at the boy, but deep down he knew the answer before his question was asked. This boy looked different, smelled different to his Jackie. Besides, it was impossible that Jackie could still be a boy after all these years . . .

The boy frowned. 'My name's not Jackie. I'm just Jack. Jack Porter.'

'Oh.' The creature sighed and

rested its head on the cave floor once
more.

Jack crept closer. 'You're a dragon,
aren't you?'

'If you say so,' the dragon replied.

'What's your name?'

The dragon snorted thick smoke out
of its nostrils. 'I used to be called Puff.
But that was long ago.'

Jack's eyes widened. 'There's a song
about you. A famous song that's been
around for years. They made us sing it at
my old school in the city.'

Puff looked interested for the first
time. 'Is there really a song about
me?'

'I wouldn't lie,' Jack said.

The dragon frowned. 'Is it a sad song?'

'It is, rather,' Jack admitted. 'It's called "Puff, the Magic Dragon". I guess that means you're magical, doesn't it?'

'You're the one telling the story,' Puff grumbled. 'Why did you wake me, anyway? I was having a lovely dream about a boy and a dragon, who meet kings and princes and fight pirates.' Puff began to cry. 'A dream about a boy and a dragon who once were friends and who will never, ever be again.'

Huge, hot tears plopped onto the stones, sizzling as they landed.

'Please don't cry,' Jack said. 'Maybe you could use your magic to find the boy again.'

Puff shook his head. 'My magic disappeared when Jackie left me.'

'Maybe I could help you get it back,' Jack said.

'No thanks.' The dragon stomped around in a circle on his nest, then settled back down with his tail to Jack. The rattling sound of dragon snores soon filled the cave.

Covering his ears against the noise, Jack left. He didn't tell Mum or Dad about Puff. He suspected they wouldn't believe him, anyway.

The next morning, Jack headed out the door with his backpack. He jogged down to the beach and across the sand to the cave at the far end. When he arrived at the entrance, he tiptoed carefully over the slippery rocks until he found the dark shape of Puff.

The dragon hadn't moved since yesterday.

'Hello!' Jack called. 'I'm back.'

He took a small, brightly coloured ball from his backpack and waved it in front of Puff's nose. 'Do you want to play fetch?'

Puff didn't move.

'How about catch? Or juggling?' Jack persisted. 'I've got loads of balls. All shapes and sizes.'

Puff snorted smoke. 'I'm not a dog. I don't "do" fetch. And I don't play catch or juggle, either.'

'You do an excellent bad mood, though,' Jack mumbled under his breath. 'How about skipping?' he said more loudly as he held up a rope. 'You could use the exercise after sleeping for so long.'

Puff groaned. 'Go away.'

'How about checkers? Or cards? I'm pretty good at Go Fish, you know.'

Puff yawned. 'Please go away or I might have to breathe fire all over you and gobble you up for a snack.'

Jack laughed suddenly. The sound echoed around the cave. 'Funny old dragon! I know you'd never do that. You might act grumpy, but deep down I think you're too kind to eat me. Well, I hope so at least.'

Puff blinked in surprise at the magical, musical sound of Jack's laughter. How he had missed it! Not that he would ever have admitted it to the pesky boy, of course.

'Why won't you play with me?' Jack said. 'It'd be fun. I promise.'

'The last boy I made friends with left me,' Puff said. 'He didn't even say goodbye. One grey night I waited and waited for him, but he never showed up. And he's never been back since. You don't know how much that hurt.'

Just like he had yesterday, Puff stomped around in a circle on his nest then settled back down with his tail to Jack.

How on earth can I heal this dragon's broken heart? Jack wondered.

That night after dinner, Jack looked up the lyrics to 'Puff, the Magic Dragon' on the internet. *What's sealing wax?* he wondered. *Oh well, I wouldn't know where to buy it, anyway. I'll have to try something else.*

After his parents went to bed, Jack snuck around the house collecting things that Puff might like, including a skull-and-crossbones flag, some pictures of autumn leaves he'd printed off the internet and some seashells – anything he could think of that might make Puff think of life outside his cave.

In the morning, he set out.

When he showed Puff all he had brought with him, the dragon snorted. 'I used to like that stuff. Not anymore. It reminds me too much of Jackie.'

Jack was suddenly angry. He'd tried being the dragon's friend, but nothing had worked. 'I've lost things too, you know,' he said.

'Like what?' Puff asked.

'I had to leave my friends behind when I moved here from the city. I had to leave behind my old house and my old school.'

'You have lost things,' Puff agreed, his face set into a hard mask of stubbornness and his dragon chin jutting out slightly. 'Now you know how I feel.'

The boy and the dragon sat in the stony silence of the cave for several minutes before Jack spoke again. 'I didn't have a choice when we moved. Mum and Dad decided for me. But I didn't go curling into a ball, crying to myself and wasting my life inside a cave, did I?'

'No,' Puff said, 'I suppose you didn't.'

'I'm trying to make the best of it,' Jack continued. 'I'm exploring everywhere and trying hard to make new friends. I'd like to be friends with you, if only you'd let me. There's fun to be had, after all, and pining for someone you've lost doesn't bring them back. So chin up, dragon.'

Puff stared at Jack for a long time. 'Where did a small boy like you learn to be so smart?'

Jack shrugged. 'My mum says it's because I eat my vegetables.' He tapped his forehead. 'Brain food, she calls it.'

Puff sighed heavily, as if letting go
of something he'd been holding inside
himself for many years. A cloud of black
smoke billowed out of his nose, causing
Jack to cough.

'Very well,' Puff said. 'I'll come
outside, though I can't promise I'll enjoy
myself.' But a smile still played on his
huge dragon lips.

Jack's face lit up as brightly as a star.
He grabbed Puff's mighty claw to make
sure he wouldn't change his mind.

'All right. Let's go.'

The dragon lumbered out of the cave towards the daylight, while Jack laughed and skipped happily beside him.

Once again, Puff couldn't help thinking how magical Jack's laughter was. Perhaps it was even more magical than he'd first thought, for if it could wake the heart of a lonely, miserable dragon, then surely it must be special.

SEA SPRITES AND ROCK POOLS

'I don't like the beach,' Holly groaned. 'It's boring.'

'It's not boring, it's fun,' Mum said.

'Boring,' Holly insisted.

Mum ran towards the waves. 'Last one in is a rotten egg!' she said, dipping her feet into the frothy sea.

Holly dawdled after her. 'The beach is

boring,' she shouted, over
the sound of the waves. 'And
I hate sand.'

'Let's build a sandcastle,'
Mum suggested. 'Then we'll see
if you still hate sand!'

'Sandcastles are boring,'
Holly said. 'I'm going for a
walk.'

'Okay, but stay
where I can see you,'
Mum said, shaking her head at Holly's
stubbornness.

Holly wandered along the beach,
keeping clear of the waves as they
stretched their wet fingers towards
her. She really didn't like the beach.

The waves were too big for her to swim in, the water was too cold and the sand was so gritty.

She came to a clump of jagged black rocks. There wasn't anything else to do so Holly climbed up and was soon standing at the top. She gazed out at the ocean for a moment but there was nothing interesting to be seen.

'Hello.'

Holly turned and saw a girl standing behind her, wearing a very unusual swimsuit. It was dark green with halter straps and a long, swishy skirt. It looked as if it were made of seaweed.

But that can't possibly be, thought Holly.

'Who are you?' Holly asked.

'I'm Serena,' the girl replied. 'What's your name?'

'Holly.'

'Do you want to explore the rock pools?' Serena asked.

Holly was tempted to say that rock pools were boring, but Serena seemed friendly and she didn't want to hurt her feelings. 'Sure, but I have to stay where Mum can see me.'

'We won't go far,' Serena said. 'Hold my hand.'

'Why?' Holly asked suspiciously.

Serena pressed her finger to her lips. 'Sh!' She smiled and took Holly's hand in hers. Then she lifted her other hand. Pointing with her index finger, she made circles above one of the rock pools and chanted:

'Ocean wild, ocean tame,

know my chant, know my name.

Hear my call, hear your daughter;

take us, now, into the water!'

Holly's body began to feel rubbery and soft. There was a strange sucking sensation in her tummy, as if she were being squeezed tight. She heard a splash . . . and realised she was treading water.

She looked up and saw black cliffs circling them. Below, fish glided through the water – fish that were bigger than she was!

'Woah!' Holly cried, her earlier

grumpiness vanishing. 'Are we *in* a rock pool?'

'We sure are,' Serena said. 'Don't you just love it?'

'B-b-but does that mean we've shrunk?' Holly shrieked. She paddled her arms and kicked her feet wildly.

Serena giggled. 'You catch on quickly. I thought you'd like to see my home up close.'

'What do you mean, your home?' Holly asked. 'And how did you shrink us?'

Serena giggled again. 'You can stop flapping your arms. You won't sink. See?' To prove her point, Serena flopped back on the water with her arms spread wide, resting there as if she were lying on a bed. 'You try it.'

'You're right,' Holly said, giving it a go. 'This is easy. But how?'

'Sea-sprite magic,' Serena said.

'What's a sea sprite?' Holly asked.

'You might know of us as mermaids,' Serena said, revealing her long, green tail and giving the water a little flick with it.

Holly stared in wonder.

'We can be any size we want,' Serena explained. 'Most of the time I swim in the ocean, but I like playing in the rock pools, too. They're fun!' She called a fish over and grasped its silver body. 'Hop onto my friend Bubbles and I'll race you.'

Holly climbed nervously onto the fish, but he was so slippery she slid straight off the other side.

'Try again,' Serena said. 'Hold on to his dorsal fin and clamp your knees tightly around his body.'

'That feels better,' Holly said.

'Great. Let's go!' Serena swam away.

Bubbles raced after her. Somehow Holly managed to stay on as Bubbles circled the rock pool, chasing Serena. The other fish joined in, leaping playfully out of the water and splashing Holly with their acrobatics.

Serena laughed as she zipped this way and that. She was very fast and an excellent swimmer. She reminded

Holly of dolphins playing at the bow of
a boat.

It was a close race, but Serena won.
Bubbles just couldn't keep up with the
energetic sea sprite.

Holly slid down off Bubbles. 'Thank
you for the ride,' she said. 'This is the
best fun I've ever had at the beach.'

Serena laughed as Bubbles splashed his tail and swam back to his friends. 'Good! Now, I've got someone else for you to meet.'

Serena introduced Holly to Snaps, the rock crab. He lived above the waterline in a rock crevice.

'Welcome,' Snaps said. 'Will you join me for some morning tea?'

Serena and Holly climbed inside Snaps's cave. The floor was covered in warm, golden sand and the rock walls were decorated with colourful seashells. Snaps was clearly very creative. And he was the perfect host. He gave them seaweed cakes to eat and seaweed tea to drink.

'These cakes are delicious,' Holly said. 'I've never tried anything like them before.'

Snaps blushed orange. 'Really? You like them? Oh, I'm so pleased! You must have another.'

After they said goodbye to Snaps, Serena asked Holly if she'd like to visit some sea stars. Serena used her magic to help Holly breathe underwater and they swam down to the bottom of the rock pool together.

The sea stars were soft and spongy to touch and were all different colours: red, orange, blue and purple. They were very cheeky, tickling each other and Holly mercilessly.

'Would you like us to teach you our special dance?' one sea star asked.

'I'd like that,' Holly said. 'I've never danced underwater before.'

The sea stars taught Holly their dance moves. She did her best to keep up with their jumping and jiving, but she tripped over her feet, knocking everyone down so that they all ended up in a colourful, exhausted, tangled heap.

Next Serena led Holly through a forest of bubbly, bobbly Neptune's necklace seaweed. Friendly red anemones waved and called out 'Hello!' as she swam past.

They came to a castle decorated with pearls and seashells.

'Wow,' Holly said. 'What a beautiful house.'

More sea sprites swam out to greet them, laughing and singing and doing somersaults.

'These are my brothers and sisters,' Serena said.

Holly played hide-and-seek, chasings and leapfrog with the sea sprites. They

were super-fast and very cheeky. Holly
had never laughed so much.

Then, in the distance, she heard a
familiar voice.

'Holly! Holly! Where have you gone
off to?'

'My mum's calling me,' she told
Serena. 'I have to go.'

'Wouldn't you like to stay with us?'
Serena said.

'I've had *so* much fun,' Holly said,
'but my mum and dad would miss me if I
didn't go home. And I'd miss them, too.'

'I understand,' Serena said. 'Will you
come back to visit?'

'Every day,' Holly said. 'I promise. But
for now, how do I get big again?'

'Hold my hand.' Serena took Holly's hand and chanted:

'Ocean wild, ocean tame,

know my chant, know my name.

Hear my call, hear your daughter;

take Holly, now, out of the water!'

A second later, a normal-sized Holly found herself standing on the rocks by the pools. She peered into the water.

Did I imagine that? she wondered.

But no. Down below – and very, very small – she could just see Serena, Serena's brothers and sisters, Snaps and Bubbles waving to her.

Holly laughed. 'See you tomorrow!' She waved goodbye to her new friends and turned to leave.

'There you are,' Mum said. 'I was getting worried. I couldn't find you.'

'Oh, you don't have to worry about me,' Holly said. 'I was checking out the rock pools. They're so cool.'

'Really?' Mum studied her. 'I thought you said the beach was boring.'

'Never! Can we come back tomorrow?'

THE PROBLEM WITH PETS

Greetings, Earthling.

My name is Kaydar. I live on a planet called Boopoolaffia. It is a long way from Earth. While I have heard of Earth and studied many of your customs, you probably would never have heard of Boopoolaffia or Boopoolaffians. That is okay. We do not mind.

(Do not be afraid! We are not planning to invade anytime soon. Or ever, in fact. We Boopoolaffians are happy living on Boopoolaffia.)

Today in class our teacher Miss Smeekle asked us to write a letter to an Earthling telling them about something interesting in our life. This is Miss Smeekle's idea of a fun activity.

Luckily I like writing and that is why you will find this letter addressed to you, Earthling most great. The interesting thing I would like to discuss with you is the problem I was having with my pet.

On Boopoolaffia, every child my age has a pet. (I am ten in Earthling years, by the way.) Pets can perform

many functions. Sometimes they fetch
toys or books or food for us. Sometimes
they help us exercise by walking with
us, jumping with us or flying with us.
Sometimes they warm us on cold nights.
Or sometimes they warn us in times
of danger – we have some rather scary
creatures on Boopoolaffia. A pet who can
protect his owner is highly valued and
well looked after.

Sometimes a pet does not do any of
these things.

And that is the problem I had with
my pet. He did not want to do anything
I tried to train him to do.

My pet was not like other pets. In fact,
he was the exact opposite of what a pet

should be. I will tell you how my problem started.

The most popular pets on Boopoolaffia are fursties. Fursties come in three colours: red, purple and blue. The most popular colour is red.

I nagged my parents for three Boopoolaffian months for a furstie. Three Boopoolaffian months is equal to about three years on Earth. That is a long time to nag someone. But I dearly wanted a red furstie and nothing else would do.

'Does it have to be a furstie?' Dad asked.

'Yes,' I said.

'Does it have to be a red furstie?' Mum asked. 'You know they are the most expensive, Kaydar.'

'Yes, Mum. It has to be a furstie that is red. That is all I want.'

Fursties are born in litters of about eight furpups. They are small and round and furry, as the name suggests.

They are cute but also needy when they are young. Fursties must be fed every three hours. If they do not get fed, they screech. Very, very loudly.

Red fursties scream the loudest.

When we brought my furstie home, he was quiet and sweet. I was over the three moons of Boopoolaffia with my choice. I decided on a name for him right away.

'I think I'll call you Cuddles,' I said as I held him tight.

Cuddles purred and snuggled up to me. I let him sleep on my pillow because he was so small and, being furry, he kept my head warm.

But over the next few months he grew. A lot. When he started taking up more room, I tried to move Cuddles to the end of my bed.

Cuddles would not have it. He loved my pillow and if I went to move him he would screech.

Soon I gave up and let him sleep where he wanted. I did not mind sleeping down the other end of the bed. It was still cosy, although a little cramped.

'I think you have spoiled him,' Mum said when she saw Cuddles sleeping on my pillow.

'He's fine,' I said from the other end of the bed.

Cuddles kept growing. He became so big he took up the entire bed. I had to sleep on the floor.

Mum and Dad talked about sending Cuddles back but I wouldn't hear of it.

'He is my furstie and I love him. I am not giving him up.'

Besides, I had already asked the lady at the furstie shop if I could give Cuddles back and she had told me they had a 'No returns' policy. 'A furstie is a pet for life,' she had said.

I asked my friends about their fursties. They all said their pets were small and cuddly and did whatever they were told to do.

My Cuddles was the only big furstie. He was also the only furstie whose feet had claws, whose head was huge and who ate all the time.

Trying to get enough food for Cuddles was almost impossible.

The only food that fursties eat
are bickleburts. Cuddles ate so many
bickleburts that I spent all my time
picking buckets of bickleburts from
the bickleburt trees in our backyard
to keep him fed.

Not only did Cuddles demand lots of
bickleburts, his behaviour got worse. If
I took him to the park, he fought with
the other fursties. He made so many
little fursties screech that my friends told
me not to bring Cuddles over for furstie
play dates anymore. I couldn't take him
anywhere!

On the day that we ran out of
bickleburts, Cuddles tried to eat me. I
had just fed him the last bickleburt from

my bucket and thought he might be full, but no. He started nibbling my antenna. I tried running away but he chased me. I had to lock myself in the bathroom so he couldn't get me.

I did not know what to do so I called the furstie doctor. He came over right away. When I heard the doorbell, I climbed out the bathroom window and let the furstie doctor into the house. He warily examined Cuddles. It didn't take long for him to give me a diagnosis.

'What you have here is not actually a furstie,' the doctor said. 'This animal only looks like a furstie when it is born. As you can see, it soon develops into something different. Something dangerous. What you have here is a gremble.'

I gulped. I had read about grembles before. On planet Earth they have things called cuckoos. You would have heard of them, I am sure. Cuckoos are birds that lay their eggs in other birds' nests. When the baby cuckoo is born, they kick the other eggs out of the nest and demand food from their adoptive parent.

Grembles are exactly like that. They will lay their eggs in a furstie nest and the furstie parents will raise the baby gremble, never realising that the baby is dangerous until it is too late. Sometimes these gremble babies are raised by furstie shop owners, way before they have grown or become dangerous.

When I went back to the furstie shop to tell the owner what had happened, she pointed out that they had a 'No refunds' policy as well as a 'No returns' policy. And, since Cuddles was hand-raised from a baby, he would not know how to fend for himself in the wild so I could not return him to the Dark Woods, where he came from, either. That would be cruel.

I was having a dilemma. I did not know what to do.

Until today when Miss Smeekle suggested I write a story to an Earthling child.

I had a great idea!

Since you on Earth know all about cuckoos and seem to be happy having them there, I thought you might have the resources to look after a gremble. Well, to be specific, my gremble, Cuddles.

So with my letter I am sending Cuddles to Earth for you to keep. I know you will be very excited about this. It is not every day that an Earthling gets to have a gremble as a pet.

I do hope he behaves better for you than he did for me. I also hope that you opened this letter before you opened the box I sent with it, so that you know exactly what you are dealing with when you see Cuddles for the first time.

I would ask you to please note that Cuddles comes with a strict 'No return to sender' policy.

From your Boopoolaffian most great friend, Kaydar Kadwallup.

ALVARADO, KING OF CATS

'Come, gather around, my kittens.'

It's a cold and snowy night. At least, outside it is. In here, beside the fire, it's warm and toasty. Exactly how we like it.

My three grandkittens lie curled at my feet, their tails tapping contentedly. It's on nights like these that my thoughts turn to Alvarado. It's been years since I saw him, but I'll never forget him.

'Listen closely, my little ones,' I say, 'and I'll tell you the story of Alvarado, King of Cats.'

Lily and Rose purr with delight. Edgeworth, ever the question-asker, pipes up, 'Was he a big cat, Grandpapa? Did he have teeth like knives and claws like razors?'

I tap Edgeworth with my paw. 'Patience. Listen, now.' He shoots me a cheeky glance before settling down again. 'All right, Grandpapa.' A hush falls and I begin.

'Alvarado was King of Cats. He was black as night and tough as they come. He was bigger than any cat I've ever seen and his teeth and claws were long and sharp. Everyone knew the legend of his adventures. And my, he was brave.

'At the time Alvarado ruled, there was a terrible war raging between the rats and the cats.

'I was born on the street, in a hole beneath the gutter. We live a life of privilege and comfort now, but the truth is that I was the child of a poor stray.

'I had to fend for myself. It was hard to find food, hard to stay warm at night. One evening while I was stealing chicken bones from a garbage bin, I heard a noise and froze. "Is anyone there?" I asked the darkness. Two red eyes glowed. I smelled something horrible. I wrinkled my nose. My whiskers twitched.

'More red eyes glowed in the darkness. Too many to count. My heart thudded in my chest. I was surrounded by rats! "Well, well, what have we here?" The Head Rat strutted towards me. He jabbed me with his filthy paw and licked his lips. "Looks like we've got dinner covered, boys."

'The other rats sniggered – and that's when it happened. A huge black cat burst into the circle of rodents, clawing, tearing, biting. Rats ran shrieking in all directions. Only the Head Rat remained.

'"What are you doing here, Jethro?" the big cat asked. "This is cat territory."

'Jethro, the Head Rat, sneered. "Not anymore. We've moved in."

'Jethro was large for sure, but no match for the cat. The enormous feline pounced and they began fighting. The noise was terrible! In the end, the rat fled – but not before he left nasty bite marks on the cat.

'"Are you all right?" I asked.

'"Of course, boy. It's just a few scratches. What's a kitten like you doing out alone, anyway?"

'I told him I'd been alone for a while and he asked me what my name was. "Regus," I said.

'He seemed surprised and peered at me in the moonlight. "Yes, so you are. I'm Alvarado. Do you know who I am?"

'Not understanding properly, I replied, "Of course I've heard of you. You're King of Cats. Surely you've better things to do than rescue stupid kittens like me."

'Alvarado laughed. "We're all worthy," he said, "whether small or big, stupid or smart, weak or strong. Come, follow me."

'Alvarado led me through dark laneways to a cellar below the slick, wet street. Waiting for us in the lair were around twenty other cats. Most were toms but a few queens were strutting around, too.

'Alvarado jumped onto an overturned milk crate to address the gathering. "Welcome everyone," he said. "We're here to discuss the war. I have discovered tonight that the rats have moved into our territory. We need to push them back and reclaim our streets."

'An old ginger cat mewed, "We're tired of fighting. When will this all end?"

'Alvarado replied firmly, "When every rat is run out of town, Ginger."

'I thought this sounded good, but another cat hissed, "Impossible! Aren't we best to make do with what they leave us?"

'"Never!" Alvarado replied. "The rats won't share the streets. They want the entire town. I say we attack and force them out, once and for all. Who will join me?"

'"I shall!" I cried.

'The other cats laughed but I noticed Alvarado watching me with pride. Ginger batted my ears. "And what are you but a weak kitten?"

'"I'm as good as any of you," I hissed fiercely. I instantly regretted my words, for I feared Ginger might attack me. But instead, he cuffed me again, more gently this time, and said, "You'll do." He then turned to Alvarado. "All right. If this milkweed is prepared to fight, so am I."

'To my surprise, many of the others soon agreed, and we began to make our plans.

'Several nights later we set out, our paws silent in the snow. I shivered, but not from the cold. It was from the anticipation of my first battle.

'It didn't take long for us to find the rats' nest. "Leave now," Alvarado told the rats. "This has always been and will always be our town."

'Jethro, the Head Rat, just laughed. Before I knew it, the battle had begun. Shrieks, hisses and squeaks erupted from both sides. We tried our best to win, but we were outnumbered. Everyone except Alvarado and I turned and ran.

'Alvarado was cornered, and twenty rats were advancing on him. I ran in, teeth and claws flying, but I was no match for the rats. They knocked me over then fell on Alvarado. I could see they weren't going to let him go. "Stop!" I scrambled to my feet. "Set him free and we'll leave right now."

'"We'll do no such thing," Alvarado argued weakly.

'Jethro's eyes swivelled to mine. "What's in it for me?" he asked.

'I told him he could have the town. All of it.

'Alvarado growled and spat, but he had no real fight left in him. He couldn't bear to look at Jethro as we retreated, but he let me drag him away, out past the last of the bright town lights and into the darkness of the surrounding countryside. "Where are you taking me?" Alvarado asked. "We've been walking for hours."

'I told him I was taking him home. When he argued that he didn't have a home, I said he soon would.

'We came to a house with a neat garden and a barn behind it. I knew it would make a good home for us. We limped through the fields towards the barn, squeezing through a hole in the timber slats. We threw ourselves down on the warm, dry straw and slept, ignoring the rumblings of the sheep and cattle inside.

'In the morning, we woke to the sound of a noisy rooster crowing. There was a scraping outside. The barn door swung open. In came two human children, a boy and a girl. When they saw us, they cleaned us up and treated us with such kindness. Their parents were kind, too. They let us stay and we were content. Or, at least I was.

'Alvarado put up with the patting and of course he loved the food. But he missed town. Once a town cat, always a town cat, I suppose.

'One dark night he slipped away. He never said goodbye, but I knew where he'd gone. His heart belonged in town. He'd never liked walking away from Jethro that night and I guess he went back to reclaim what was his.'

'Do you think he's still King of Cats?' Lily asks. 'Do you think he rules the town again?'

I sigh as I struggle to pull myself out of my memories and into the present. How can I tell her that Alvarado left so long ago that he is probably in Cat Heaven now?

Instead, I smile and say, 'Alvarado will always

be King of Cats. Now, bedtime, my
kittens.'

With a quiet purr, we snuggle
together for the night. As my
grandkittens fall asleep beside me in the
comfort of the farmhouse, I stare out
at the snow falling and I remember big,
brave Alvarado.

My father.

King of Cats.

DINO-GIRL

Daisy stepped carefully onto the bus. She looked left and right. She looked behind her.

There was no sign of Alice.

Sighing with relief, Daisy ran up the last few steps, down the narrow aisle, and dived into the first empty seat she came to. She sat back and gazed out the window, trying to make herself as small as possible so that none of the kids running past would notice her.

Daisy was invisible.

Almost.

'Hey Dino-Girl!' Alice pinched Daisy's arm as she fell into the seat beside her.

'Ouch,' Daisy gasped. 'That hurt.' She rubbed her arm and leaned towards the window, but Alice only moved closer.

'Don't you have somewhere else to sit?' Daisy asked. *There, I said it*, Daisy thought. *I spoke up this time.*

'No,' Alice said, her voice as sugary-sweet as her smile. 'I don't. Why do you like dinosaurs so much, Dino-Girl?'

Everyone knew Daisy was into dinosaurs. She had lots of books about dinosaurs and often brought them to school for news. And whenever it was uniform-free day, she wore her shirt with the T. rex on it.

Daisy shrugged. She didn't want to answer Alice, but she was afraid she might get another pinch if she didn't. 'Dinosaurs are interesting.'

'No they're not. Anyone who likes dinosaurs is boring,' Alice teased, leaning in close to Daisy and breathing all over her. 'And you *love* dinosaurs so you must be super-boring!'

Daisy swallowed hard. 'At least I don't have stinky breath,' she said, wrinkling her nose.

She knew she shouldn't have said anything, but she was trying so hard to stay strong against Alice's constant mean words. Alice's breath was really gross. It was the only thing Daisy could think of to say to defend herself.

'Why, you little rat!' said Alice. She pinched Daisy's arm again, harder this time.

'Ouch!' Daisy yelped. It took her all her strength not to cry.

'*Alice Little.*' The girls looked up to see their teacher, Mrs Woolly, frowning at them. 'I saw what you did. Go to the back of the bus right now.'

Alice growled at Daisy then trotted to the back of the bus where, unknown to Mrs Woolly, her friends were waiting for her. She high-fived each of them before sitting down.

Mrs Woolly squeezed into the seat beside Daisy.

'Are you all right?' Mrs Woolly asked.

'I'm okay.' Daisy rubbed her arm. She tried to smile and sound brave. 'Alice doesn't bother me.'

'Good girl. Don't let her get to you,' Mrs Woolly said. She leaned back in her seat. 'You must be excited about this special dinosaur exhibit. I heard it's the biggest in the country.'

Daisy nodded. 'It is. And did you know that the museum has a research centre where they study dinosaur DNA? They're hoping to clone a T. rex one day.'

When they arrived at the museum, it took Alice less than three minutes to find Daisy. 'Hey Dino-Girl, where's the woolly mammoth?'

'This is a dinosaur exhibit, Alice. There aren't any woolly mammoths.'

'You know who I mean. That old fossil, Mrs Woolly.'

I wish she would go away! Daisy thought. She walked towards a

Chasmosaurus skeleton and pretended to read the information sign.

'What were you two talking about, anyway?' Alice asked.

'Nothing.'

'Don't lie. I saw you two talking. Did you say anything about our game of chase last Friday?'

'It wasn't a game,' Daisy said, remembering how scared she'd been when Alice had chased her down the street on her way home from school. At one stage, she'd had to run across the busy road so Alice wouldn't catch her.

'*Did you say anything?*' Alice hissed.

'No,' Daisy murmured as she studied her feet in shame. She didn't like being scared of Alice, but what could she do? Alice was bigger and meaner than Daisy could ever be.

'Good.' Alice pushed Daisy, causing her to drop her backpack.

Daisy felt a sudden rush of anger. *Why does Alice have to ruin everything?* 'Please leave me alone,' she said, trying to sound really firm.

'Who's going to make me?' Alice reached out to pinch Daisy's arm.

Daisy dodged just in time and scurried down the hallway. Alice chased after her.

The hallway curved to the right then came to a dead end. The only way out was a door on Daisy's left. It was marked

'LABORATORY: NO PUBLIC ACCESS'.
Daisy heard footsteps coming from
behind. She had no choice. She opened
the door a fraction and slipped in,
hoping Alice hadn't seen or heard her
go inside.

Benches of microscopes and light
boxes lined the lab walls. In one corner,
a desk was piled high with papers and
instruments. On the far wall was a
whiteboard covered with lots of numbers
and letters. In the middle of the room

sat a huge, strange-looking egg-shaped capsule with dials and buttons on it. It was so big it almost touched the ceiling.

The door handle rattled behind Daisy.

Oh, no! Where can I hide? She looked around. *Not under the desk, Alice will see me . . .*

The only place big enough was the capsule. Daisy opened the door and leapt inside. *Ha! She'll never find me in here!*

In her panic, she didn't notice the sign 'DINO FUSION CHAMBER' on the outside of the capsule.

Just as Daisy started to calm down, she heard the capsule door lock with a heavy click. She peeked out the capsule window and saw Alice staring right at her.

'I've got you now, Dino-Girl,' she said, grinning.

Daisy was frightened. She didn't want to be locked in the capsule. What if Alice didn't let her out? How would Mrs Woolly find her?

'Open up!' Daisy banged on the door.

'Relax, Dino-Girl. I'm just having a bit of fun.' Alice laughed, turning dials and pressing rows and rows of buttons, running her hand along them as if she were playing a piano.

'Don't do that! What if something happens?'

The capsule began to rattle and hum. Alice suddenly looked scared. 'Wait! Stop!' She punched more buttons. The humming grew louder. Alice jumped back in fright. 'Stop! I didn't mean it!'

Daisy didn't hear her. The capsule was making too much noise. And strange things were happening. Her skin rippled. Her head grew and stretched . . .

'Help!' Daisy cried. She didn't want to see what was happening. She shut her eyes and wished for it all to be over.

After a few moments the rattling and humming stopped. Everything went still and quiet. Daisy took a deep breath. Slowly, she opened her eyes and looked around. The capsule seemed smaller . . . Or was she bigger?

Daisy stared at her hands. They still looked like her hands, but now they were brown and bumpy and covered with scales and her fingernails were long and yellow, like claws.

Her legs were scaly, too, and very, very muscly.

Her feet were so big they had burst right out of her school shoes.

Daisy's hand groped the air behind her. Then she felt it: a long, scaly, bumpy tail!

Daisy looked up and saw her reflection in the capsule window. Her eyes looked the same but her face was quite different. For one thing, she didn't have a nose anymore, she had a snout. And instead of small, even, human teeth, her mouth was full of huge, sharp *dinosaur* teeth.

She wasn't just a girl anymore. She was a dinosaur, too. Half girl, half dinosaur. She really *was* Dino-Girl!

Daisy smiled, thinking of all the wonderful things she could do now that she was part dinosaur. How strong she would be! How fast she would be able to run!

No one would tease her ever again. Dino-Girl burst out of the capsule.

Stepping over the wreckage, she strode towards Alice, who was pressed up against the lab door, her eyes wide with fear.

'Look what you've done!' Dino-Girl said, but to Alice it sounded like a scary roar.

'I'm s-s-sorry,' Alice stuttered. 'Don't hurt me!'

Dino-Girl smiled, her tail swishing from side to side. 'Oh, I won't hurt you, Alice,' she said, 'but I *am* going to enjoy playing chase with you! *RAAAAGGGGHHHH!*

SWOOP

'What is it, Kasey?'

Mum peered at the tiny creature in Kasey's cupped hands.

'A baby magpie.' Kasey peered up into the branches of the gum tree towering above her in the backyard. 'He must have fallen out of his nest. Can we keep him?'

Mum shook her head. 'We've got so many other animals to look after. How will we find time to care for a baby bird?'

Kasey lived on a farm with her parents. They certainly had plenty of animals: a herd of milking cows, two quarrelsome bulls, a handful of horses plus seven goats, twelve laying hens, four dogs and three cats. But a magpie was different. *Special.* No one else had a magpie for a pet. They were wild animals, not like all the other animals you'd find on a farm.

'I'll feed him,' said Kasey. 'Every day. I promise.'

'I don't know,' Mum said uncertainly.

'Pretty please with sugar on top?'

Mum laughed as she shook her head. 'Oh, all right. But I hope you're up to the job, young lady. Babies take a lot of looking after, you know!'

'Oh, I'm up to it. Thanks, Mum!' Kasey's grin stretched right across her face.

Kasey carried the bird into the house. She filled an old shoebox with torn-up newspaper and gently placed the magpie inside. The magpie fixed her with his marble eyes. He blinked at her once. Twice. Then he tilted his head back and started shrieking. The sound was like a rusty pair of scissors opening and shutting again and again.

'Uh-oh. I think he's hungry,' Kasey said. 'What can I feed him?'

'I've got just the thing.' Mum poured some rolled oats, honey and warm milk into a bowl, mashing it up until the mixture was soft and runny. 'We should feed him what he would eat in the wild, but unless you want to chew worms and vomit them up again, this will have to do.'

'Gross,' Kasey said.

'We'll use this to feed him.' Mum offered Kasey an eye-dropper from an old medicine bottle. 'Do you want to try?'

'Sure.'

'Slowly, now,' Mum instructed. 'He's only little and doesn't know when to stop.'

Kasey squeezed the oat mixture into the magpie's gaping mouth. 'He likes it,' she said, as the baby bird drank eagerly.

'Have you thought of a name yet?' Mum asked.

'Swoop.'

'Perfect. That way it doesn't matter if he's a boy or she's a girl. The name suits either one.'

Kasey didn't say anything but she was sure that Swoop was a boy. She could just tell.

Kasey kept her word and fed Swoop every day. She loved looking after the

magpie and Swoop clearly loved Kasey.
He always squawked happily when she
walked into the room and when she held
her finger out to him, he would jump
straight on.

Swoop grew quickly. Kasey started to
feed him fresh minced meat to make
him strong and healthy. In no time at
all, the
magpie's
fluffy down
fell out and
was replaced by grey, faded-looking
feathers.

Soon after that, Swoop got his
grown-up feathers. He was as sleek and
shiny as a moonlit night, with black

and white in all the right places. Kasey noticed that some of Swoop's feathers were a little greyer on his neck. She borrowed some books from the library and discovered that the grey on his neck meant that Swoop was a girl, not a boy!

As she grew older, Swoop became more adventurous. Sometimes she would disappear all day and only return home at dusk to eat the food Kasey left out for her. Then she would leave again.

Kasey couldn't help wondering where she went.

'Why doesn't she stay home with me?' Kasey complained.

'She's a wild bird,' Mum said. 'She probably sees other magpies around and is learning from them. She loves you, I'm sure, but she also wants her freedom.'

'But she never comes when I call! The only time she comes home is to eat.'

Mum hugged Kasey. 'Be happy she comes home. That has to count for something.'

But Kasey didn't like it when Swoop disappeared. When she came home to eat at dusk, Kasey started locking her in a cage she had on the front porch, to keep her there for the night. She tried to remember to let Swoop out in the morning but sometimes, in her rush to get to school, Kasey forgot. Then poor Swoop would sit in her cage all day, clutching her wings to her sides and watching sadly as the other magpies called to her from the sky.

Swoop started coming home less and less. Kasey became moody and couldn't concentrate at school, especially when Lily McDonald from next door told her that Swoop often dropped by her house to steal the cat's food.

Kasey wanted to tell Lily she was wrong, that Swoop would never prefer Lily's place to hers. She wanted to tell Lily to mind her own business and to stop stealing other people's pets. She wanted to poke her tongue out at Lily and pull horrible faces . . . But she didn't because she knew it wouldn't change anything between her and Swoop.

One evening as the sun was going down, Kasey sat outside, waiting and watching for Swoop to show up. When it became dark and Swoop still hadn't come home, Kasey ran inside and threw herself on her bed.

She cried and cried, her heart breaking with the knowledge that Swoop didn't need her anymore.

'You have to learn to let go, Kasey,' Mum said when she found her. 'Sometimes that's what being a mum means.'

Kasey looked up with red, swollen eyes. 'But I love her so much! I just want to be with her.'

'Swoop loves you too, darling. You'll

always be her mum. But she's grown-up now. It's best to let her come and go as she pleases, otherwise she won't want to come home at all.'

Kasey thought about what Mum said. The next evening she put Swoop's favourite minced meat on her feeding post. Then she went inside and watched from the kitchen window, waiting patiently for Swoop to arrive.

When Swoop came, Kasey let her feed for a while, then went out to her.

Swoop immediately stopped eating and tilted her head to watch Kasey warily. Tears pricked Kasey's eyes. There had been a time when Swoop would come to her eagerly. Now she didn't seem to trust her at all.

Kasey glanced at the cage, feeling terrible. 'Don't worry.' She stroked Swoop's silky feathers one last time. 'I won't put you in that stupid cage again. You're all grown-up now, so I'm letting you go. Just remember that I love you and to visit me now and then.'

Swoop tilted her black head at Kasey and warbled happily, as if she understood Kasey perfectly. Then, with a crisp flap of her wings, like an umbrella bursting open, she took to the sky. In a moment she was gone, her dark shape blending into the twilight.

Kasey stopped putting food out for Swoop. She stopped calling for her and she put Swoop's cage away. She tried not

to worry about her or to miss her too
much, though it wasn't easy to do.

But no matter what, Kasey always kept
one eye on the sky.

Just in case.

Then late one spring, Kasey heard a
familiar warbling.

'Swoop's back!' she cried as she ran
outside.

Kasey saw a large magpie with
feathers as sleek and shiny as a moonlit
night and with black and white and grey
in all the right places. Hopping about on

the lawn with the grown-up magpie were two faded, grey-speckled youngsters.

The grown-up magpie warbled merrily to Kasey. Then she strode over to her babies to share a worm with them.

Kasey's heart bubbled with happiness. 'I missed you so much, Swoop! Thanks for bringing your babies back to see me. They look just like you.'

THE IVORY PONY

'Good morning!' Bella trilled as she
burst into her parents' bedroom. She
ran to the windows and threw back the
curtains. The sun was barely peeping
through the mountains to the east.
'Mummy! Daddy! Wake up! It's time!
The day is finally here!'

Queen Ruby groaned, snuggling
deeper beneath the coverlet. 'Bella, it's
too early. Have patience, child.'

'Patience?' Bella squeaked. 'I've waited ten years for this day and you and Daddy promised. Zara has one and so does Maddy. It's my turn, now, so please get up!'

A sleepy King Brune rolled over. 'I'm certain that princesses aren't meant to be so bossy,' he said, yawning. 'Hold onto your horses, Bella. We're coming.' He rose and pulled on his socks and shirt. A smile twitched on his lips at his daughter's excitement.

'It's not every day a girl gets her own winged pony, Daddy. Hurry, now. The maids have breakfast ready.'

Queen Ruby slid out of bed. She slipped into her dressing-gown and hugged Bella. 'Happy birthday, darling. I suppose the celebrations will have to wait until you return.'

Bella nodded. 'This is the one time I don't mind waiting for my cake.'

'Right. I'm ready,' King Brune said.

Bella clapped her hands with delight then dragged her parents downstairs.

The dining-room fire was warm and welcoming. Bella's sisters Zara and Maddy were already there, scoffing freshly baked raspberry muffins.

'Happy birthday, little sister!' they cried as Bella walked in. Bella hugged them both, glad they had risen early to see her off.

King Brune headed straight for the bacon and eggs while Bella nibbled marmalade toast. She was so excited she could hardly eat, but she knew she had to. It would be a difficult walk along a steep track to the top of Mount Valour where the winged ponies grazed.

Still, the walk up Mount Valour would be the easiest part of today's test. It was the thought of what came after that which made Bella's tummy flip nervously. Once at the top, Princess Bella could select one – and only one – winged pony from the herd. Then she would have to call the pony to her and hope that it accepted her. If it did, the pony would be hers forever, just as royal tradition decreed.

If she failed . . . Well, Bella didn't want to think about that.

Seeing that her dad had finished eating, Bella said goodbye to her mum and her sisters and hurried King Brune out the door. She chatted constantly, trying to forget her nerves.

After several hours, Bella threw herself on the ground, puffing and sweating. 'This is harder than I thought it would be,' she gasped.

King Brune paused to lean on a boulder and have a moment's rest. He handed Bella the water pouch. 'Shall we turn back?' he asked, his eyes twinkling with mischief.

Bella took a refreshing drink of water. 'Never!'

King Brune laughed. 'I was hoping you'd say that. Let's keep going.'

Bella and King Brune reached the summit at noon. The sun shone brightly on the thick grass, which was dotted with crimson wildflowers. Bella could tell right away that this was a magical place. There was a feeling of peace and calm on the mountain that was different to anything Bella had ever felt before.

Bella looked around, searching for the winged ponies. Where were they? She panicked for a moment before she spotted the herd in the distance. When they weren't flying across the heavens,

this was the only place they came
to graze.

'Time to choose,' King Brune said
as they strolled towards the herd.
'Remember: be certain of your choice. If
the pony you choose refuses to be tamed,
you'll miss out. No second chances.'

Bella gulped. She couldn't bear the
thought of failing, or the thought that
her sisters might have winged ponies and
she wouldn't. It had happened before.
She'd heard of it in the old legends.

That would be the worst thing ever, Bella
thought.

The ponies were the most beautiful
creatures she'd ever seen. Some were
dappled grey. Others were as black as

the feathers of a crow or as pale as the pebbles at Ash Bay. Some had honey-gold coats. Others were rusty brown. All were tall and muscular, with sweeping manes and tails and huge wings, which they would occasionally flap as they munched on the grass.

They're all so achingly beautiful! Bella thought. *And yet none seem quite right.*

Then Bella spotted her.

Nibbling contentedly near a group of pine trees was an ivory-coloured pony with a charcoal-grey mane, tail and wings. As if sensing Bella watching her, the pony lifted her head to stare at the girl before returning to her grazing.

Bella's breath caught in her throat.

'That's her,' she whispered, pointing the pony out.

'She's a beauty,' King Brune said. 'Now try to call her to you.'

Bella's heart pounded against her rib cage. She took a step towards the pony. Then another. And another.

At first the mare remained unmoving except for an occasional swish of her tail. But as Bella got closer, the mare trotted away.

Bella swallowed her disappointment. She took a deep breath and walked towards the pony again, cooing gently, 'Here, my lovely, here.'

This time, the mare fluttered off, only to land a short distance away.

Bella's hopes sank. *I've chosen the wrong one.*

'What should I do?' Bella's shoulders sagged. 'She keeps going away.'

'She's a wild pony, remember?' King Brune said. 'She'll only connect with a girl she feels she can trust. Is there something special about you that you can show her?'

There's nothing special about me, Bella thought. But she wouldn't give up. Instead, she lifted her face to the sun, waiting for a clue, a sign, that might tell her how to win over the ivory pony.

Suddenly, a jolt of heat rushed through her. She felt the energy of the magic that swirled through this secret

place. She closed her eyes and listened
to the breeze chattering in the trees.
She was certain it was trying to tell her
something.

Finally, she heard it: the soft, lilting
strains of a familiar tune.

Bella opened her eyes and smiled.
She knew what to do.

Carefully, so as not to frighten her,
Bella faced the mare and began singing
the lullaby her mum had sung to her
when she was a baby. Even though she
was now ten, it was still Bella's favourite
song. It always made her feel calm, safe
and loved.

'Come sit with me, my darling,
    and listen to my song.

Come sit with me, my darling;

we'll snuggle all night long.

I'll hold you close to my heart,

its beat is sure and true.

Yes, I'll hold you close to my heart,

forever loving you.'

As Bella finished her song, the pony

took a cautious step towards her.

It's working! Bella thought. She kept

singing.

'Come sit with me, my darling . . .'

When Bella had sung the lullaby for

the third time, the pony was so close that

Bella could almost touch her. Girl and

pony stood face to face in the sunlit field,

the breeze whispering around them, the

grass shivering at their feet.

Bella's mouth was dry with fear. She swallowed hard.

Please, please, please, she chanted in her mind.

The beautiful, shy, ivory pony stretched out her nose. Bella lifted her hand, palm up. The pony nuzzled Bella's hand. She stepped closer again until Bella was able to wrap her arms around the pony's neck and bury her face deep in her mane to drink in her rich, horsey smell.

This was the moment Bella had dreamed of.

This was the moment Bella would remember forever.

Now she had her very own winged pony and nothing – *nothing* – would ever be the same again.

'Will you let me ride you, Shy One?' Bella whispered.

The ivory pony nickered and, to Bella's amazement, knelt down. Bella eased her leg over the mare's back, careful not to hurt her wings, and held on gently to the mare's mane.

Bella glanced at King Brune, who stood watching her with tears in his eyes.

She gave him the thumbs up. 'I did it, Daddy!'

'You sure did,' King Brune replied proudly.

With a flap of her mighty wings, the pony rose into the air, carrying Bella with her.

'Fly, Shy One!' Bella urged her ivory pony. 'Fly!'

THE THREE LITTLE LAMBS AND THE BIG BAD CHICKEN

Once upon a time there lived three little lambs.

The first little lamb lived in a house made of straw. The second little lamb lived in a house made of sticks. The third little lamb lived in a house made of bricks. The three little brothers lived on Woolstock Farm and were very content until one day when the Big Bad Chicken came to visit.

The Big Bad Chicken had a reputation for being big. She stood taller than any barn or wheat silo. When she flapped her wings she created tornado-like wind currents. Her feet had long, sharp claws that scratched and scraped and she clucked so loudly it could make your ears ache.

The Big Bad Chicken also had a reputation for being bad. She stomped about the countryside, stepping on buildings, scratching up crops and trees and taking no notice of who or what got in her way. Her beak was razor sharp and she loved sticking it in places where a beak shouldn't be stuck.

When she wandered onto Woolstock Farm while out for her morning walk, the Big Bad Chicken caused a dreadful stir.

She was feeling rather unwell because she had a big bad cold. Her nostrils were runny, her eyes were itchy and her throat was sore.

When the Big Bad Chicken spotted a golden-yellow pile of straw sitting in the sun, she clucked, 'How delightful!' and ran over for a closer look.

The first little lamb was not happy to see the Big Bad Chicken on his doorstep. 'Go away, Big Bad Chicken, or I'll bleat and I'll bunt and I'll knock you over.'

The Big Bad Chicken was upset by the little lamb's words. 'You'll do no

such thing,' she said, before doing the
biggest, baddest sneeze ever heard.
Achoooooooooooooooooo!

The Big Bad Chicken's sneeze blew
the first little lamb's house to pieces.
The first little lamb was very cross. He
was all set to bleat and bunt the Big Bad
Chicken, but his brothers stopped him.

'It was an accident,' the second little
lamb said. As sorry as he was for his

brother, the second little lamb had been taught to always think the best of people. He knew the Big Bad Chicken couldn't help having a cold. 'It's clear what's going on here. I have an idea.' And he told his brothers what they should do.

The three little lambs went to their orchard and picked boxes full of lemons. Then they gathered around the fireplace in the second little lamb's house. They picked up their knitting needles and, using the wool off their own backs, knitted a special piece of clothing.

In the morning they visited the Big Bad Chicken in the valley behind their farm.

'Good morning,' the first little lamb said. 'We made this to help keep you warm.' He handed her a bright woollen scarf. 'We also prepared this hot lemon drink to soothe your sore throat, so that your cold might go away.'

Clucking with happiness, the Big Bad Chicken wrapped the scarf around her neck and sipped the lemon drink. 'This is delicious,' she said. 'Thank you, you're very kind.'

The three little lambs skipped back to their farm. The first little lamb went to live with his older brother in the stick house and looked forward to everything returning to normal.

But later that day, the Big Bad Chicken came scratching around Woolstock Farm again. When she spied a neatly stacked pile of dried worms, she clucked, 'How delightful!' and ran over for a closer look.

The second little lamb was not happy to see the Big Bad Chicken on his doorstep. 'Go away, Big Bad Chicken, or I'll bleat and I'll bunt and I'll knock you over.'

The Big Bad Chicken was upset by the little lamb's words. 'You'll do no such thing,' she said, pecking at the little lamb's house and gobbling up all the sticks until there was nothing left.

The second little lamb was very cross. He was all set to bleat and bunt the Big Bad Chicken, but his brothers stopped him.

'She didn't mean it,' the third little lamb said. As sorry as he was for his brother, the third little lamb had been taught to always think the best of people. He knew the Big Bad Chicken couldn't help being hungry. 'It's clear what's going on here. I have an idea.' And he told his brothers what they should do.

The three little lambs wheeled their wagons to the grain stores. They worked all night, filling the wagons with wheat, sunflower seeds and corn.

In the morning they visited the Big Bad Chicken.

'Good morning,' the second little lamb said. 'We've brought you some food so you won't be so hungry anymore.'

They tipped the wheat, sunflower seeds and corn into neat piles for the Big Bad Chicken to eat.

'Oh, my!' cried the Big Bad Chicken, pecking at the grain. 'What lovely food. Thank you, you're very kind.'

'Problem solved,' the third little lamb said as he and his brothers headed home with their empty wagons. 'The Big Bad Chicken isn't so bad after all. She was just hungry.'

The first and second little lambs went to live with their older brother in his brick house. They thought all would return to normal, but at noon the Big Bad Chicken showed up again.

She was feeling much better because of the scarf, the hot lemon drink and the food. Still, she felt an urge deep inside her. Something was not quite right.

When she spied a clean, dry roost, high up off the ground, she clucked, 'How delightful!' and ran over for a closer look.

The third little lamb was not happy to see the Big Bad Chicken on his doorstep. 'Go away, Big Bad Chicken, or I'll bleat and I'll bunt and I'll knock you over.'

The Big Bad Chicken was upset by the little lamb's words. 'You'll do no such thing,' she said. Then she ruffled her feathers, sat on top of the third little lamb's brick house, poked her head under her wing and fell fast asleep.

But the roof shingles and beams and walls creaked and cracked, shattering under her weight.

The third little lamb was very cross. He was all set to bleat and bunt the Big Bad Chicken, but his brothers stopped him.

'It's lovely that she thought your house would make a comfortable roost. It was only bad luck that she was too heavy,' the first little lamb said. As sorry as he was for his brother – and as much as he knew exactly how his brother felt because he too had lost his house – the first little lamb had been taught to always think the best of people. 'It's clear what's going on here. I have an idea.' And he told his brothers what they should do.

The three little lambs travelled into town. They came to a shop with a sign that said 'Carpenter' out the front. Inside, they found an old man bent over his workbench.

'Dear Geppetto,' said the first little lamb, 'the Big Bad Chicken is short-sighted. We were hoping you could make her some spectacles to help her see better.'

'Certainly,' Geppetto said. 'The glassmaker next door can help me.'

Geppetto and the glassmaker worked all night. In the morning, the three little lambs carried the giant spectacles home on a hay wagon. They found the Big Bad Chicken still sitting on what was left of the third little lamb's brick house.

The third little lamb gently prodded her awake. 'Good morning,' he said. 'We have something for you.'

'For me?' clucked The Big Bad Chicken. 'How delightful!'

The three little lambs handed her the spectacles. 'Rest them on your beak,' they instructed her.

The Big Bad Chicken peered through the spectacles, flapping her wings in excitement.

'Oh my goodness!' she cried when she saw the ruins of the brick house beneath her. 'Have I been sitting on your house? I do apologise. I thought it was a nest. Without these spectacles, I haven't been able to see properly. I've been such a clumsy, silly chicken. Can you forgive me?'

'Of course,' said the kind little lambs together.

The Big Bad Chicken was overcome with gratitude . . . and something else rather different altogether. She gave a squawk and before she knew it, she had laid a giant egg.

The egg fell to the ground.

Right on top of the three little lambs, covering them in sticky, yellow yolk.

'Oh well,' the first little lamb said, sighing. 'They do say egg yolk makes your wool smooth and silky.'

ABOUT THE AUTHOR

Aleesah Darlison is a much-published award-winning Australian author. She has written over twenty picture books and novels for boys and girls of all ages. The themes in her stories promote the concepts of courage, understanding, anti-bullying, love, self-belief, friendship and teamwork. Her books include *Spider Iggy*, *Little Meerkat*, *Puggle's Problem*, *Warambi*, *Little Good Wolf*, *Ash Rover* and the Unicorn Riders series. Most recently, Aleesah won the 2015 Environment Award for Children's Literature in the nonfiction category for her book *Our Class Tiger*. When Aleesah isn't creating entertaining and enchanting stories for children, she's usually looking after her four energetic children or taking her frisky dog, Floyd, for long walks on the beach. Her website is www.aleesahdarlison.com

ABOUT THE ILLUSTRATOR

James Hart is an illustrator, comic artist and avid doodler living in the Melbourne area with his wife, kids and dog called Shasta, who is terribly afraid of the wind and butterflies. As a kid, James was raised on a healthy diet of comics, video games, cartoons, action figures and Lego. Since beginning his journey as an illustrator in 2003 he has worked on many different projects, from toy design to book illustration. Recent projects include the animated TV series *The Day My Butt Went Psycho* and the You Choose books by George Ivanoff. When he's not drawing his favourite things (aliens, robots and monsters) he's being a dad and husband, watching movies and cartoons, drinking coffee, listening to music, reading . . . and drinking coffee. James' website is www.jameshart.com.au

OUT NOW